For Danny, Marc and Ryan Strinkas

Kevin's Magic Ring was published in March 1989 by Black Moss Press
of 1939 Alsace Ave., Windsor, Ontario, Canada N8W1M5.

Kevin's Magic Ring is published with the assistance of the Canada Council
and the Ontario Arts Council.

Black Moss Books are distributed in Canada and the U.S. by Firefly Books
of Scarborough, Ontario, Canada. All orders should be directed there.

This book was designed by Jirina Marton.
It was printed by The National Press, Toronto, Canada.

ISBN 0-88753-188-1

Kevin's Magic Ring

Written by Patricia Quinlan
Illustrated by Jirina Marton

Black Moss Press

In the corner of Kevin's attic was a magician's trunk that once belonged to his Great Uncle Marcus. In the trunk was a large picture of Uncle Marcus performing magic tricks at a country fair.

Kevin liked to do magic too. One day, he dressed up in Uncle Marcus' hat and cloak. He tried to make a coin disappear. As he pulled a large red handkerchief from one of the pockets, a key fell to the floor.

When Kevin looked at the key, he remembered a small box in the bottom of the trunk. The box was locked and no one had been able to open it.

Kevin held his breath as he turned the key in the lock. When he opened the box, he saw a ring and a note. The note said:

> **The power of the magic ring is given for only three days. To receive the power of the ring, you must believe that the impossible is possible and recite the magic words while looking at the brightest star in the sky.**

It was signed, "Marcus the Magnificent."

Kevin looked closely at the ring. The words, "ah choo, ah choo" were engraved on the inside of the band. They must be the magic words! he thought. Kevin could hardly wait for the night to come.

When it was dark, Kevin went outside. He put the ring on his finger and looked for the brightest star. I believe the impossible is possible, he thought. Then he said the magic words, "ah choo! ah choo!"

"Kevin, you're catching a cold," his mother shouted, "you'd better come in and get your jacket."

Kevin waited for something unusual to happen, but at first nothing did.

The next day, Kevin was standing at the corner of Greenwood Avenue waiting for the light to change. He was trying to decide between buying a chocolate chip or a cherry vanilla ice cream cone. The woman beside him was wearing a strong perfume.

"A-a-ah-cho-o-o!" Kevin sneezed.
Suddenly, a bus, a van, four cars, and a girl walking her dog all stopped.

Kevin waved his hand in front of the woman beside him. She didn't even blink. "A-a-ah cho-o-o!" Kevin sneezed again. "What are you waving at me for?" the woman asked. "Wow! It must be the power of the ring!" Kevin shouted. He forgot all about buying ice cream and ran home.

Kevin tried to tell his parents about the magic ring during dinner.

"That's very interesting," his mom said, "now eat your broccoli. It has vitamins."

"When I was a boy, I used to do magic tricks," his dad said.

"A-a-ah-cho-o-o!" Kevin sneezed. Everything stopped.Kevin's magic cat Sneakers was jumping from the counter. He looked like he was frozen in mid air.

"Ah-a-ah-cho-o-o!" Kevin sneezed again.

"Your cold's getting worse," his mother said, "you'd better go to bed early."

That night, Kevin lay awake thinking about the power of the ring. I get it. When I say "ah choo" the first time, everything stops. When I say "ah choo" the second time, everything starts again.

I could be a hero, Kevin thought. He imagined the mayor giving him an award for stopping a plane crash and saving hundreds of people. Or maybe I'll be rich. Some one might pay a million dollars for the magic ring.

Kevin fell asleep thinking about the things he would buy . . . a new bike, 100 pounds of jelly beans, 1,000 comic books, a computer for his mom and a video camera for his dad.

The next morning, Kevin went shopping with his mom.

"Can we buy some jelly beans? he asked.

"Kevin, you know jelly beans aren't good for you. They rot your teeth," she said.

"A-a-ah-cho-o-o!" Kevin said, pretending to sneeze. Everything stopped. While his mother stood holding a cucumber, Kevin scooped some jelly beans out of the bin. He hid the bag under a large box of oatmeal in the bottom of the cart.

"A-a-ah-cho-o-o!" Kevin pretended to sneeze again. His mother put the cucumber in the cart and headed for the check out counter. She was reading a magazine and didn't notice as the jelly beans landed in the shopping bag.

When they got home, Kevin grabbed the jelly beans when his mom wasn't looking. He ate the whole bag and got a terrible stomach ache.

Later that afternoon, Kevin was playing football. The score was seven to three and Kevin's team was losing. The game was almost over.

"A-a-ah-cho-o-o" Kevin said, pretending to sneeze. Everything stopped. Kevin grabbed the ball and ran for the goal line. "A-a-ah-cho-o-o!" Kevin said again just before he scored a touch down.

Kevin's team won and he was the hero of the game.

Later, Kevin tried to tell his friends, Danny and Ryan, what really happened.

"I don't believe you. You're just fooling us," Danny said.
"But it's true," Kevin insisted.
"Prove it! Ryan said.

Kevin couldn't think of a way to prove it. He began to feel very alone with this strange power that no one else could understand.

That night, Kevin had trouble sleeping. There was only one more day and then the power of the ring would be gone. He wished he could do something very special with the power of the magic ring.

The next day, Kevin was watching a mother bird teaching her baby bird how to fly. The baby bird lost its balance and fell to the ground. Sneakers saw what happened and was about to pounce.

"Ah choo!" Kevin said quickly.   Everything stopped.   Kevin lifted the baby bird carefully and put it back into the nest.

"Ah choo!" Kevin said again.
He laughed because Sneakers
looked very confused.

The next morning Kevin was playing marbles. "A-a-ah cho-o-o!" Kevin sneezed. Nothing happened. Kevin felt sad because the power of the ring was gone.

A few minutes later, Kevin heard a sound and looked up. He smiled when he saw the baby bird flying with his mother.